W9-AGW-505

The Dog Who Came to Visit

The Dog
Who Came
To Visit

by IRMENGARDE EBERLE

Illustrated by Roger Payne

Abelard-Schuman
London   New York   Toronto

London	*New York*	*Toronto*
Abelard-Schuman	Abelard-Schuman	Abelard-Schuman
Limited	Limited	Canada Limited
8 King St. WC2	6 West 57th St.	896 Queen St. W.

Printed in the United States of America

By the same author
  Pete and the Mouse
  The Raccoon's Young Ones

Contents

The Dog Who Came to Visit

1

A Double Surprise

It was Saturday, and it had been raining all morning. Sandra Allen stood by the living room window and looked out at the street.

All was quiet. No one was out today except the boxer, Sally, who was trotting toward her home down the block. She looked miserable, because she didn't like the rain in her face.

Sandra ran to the door. "Come in, Sally," she called, "and stay till the rain stops."

She was always trying to get the neighborhood dogs to come to her house for a little visit.

The dog came to her now, and Sandra hugged her, wet as she was. Then she pulled her gently by the collar till they were in front of her father, who was reading.

"Look, isn't this a nice dog?" she said.

"Yes," said Mr. Allen. "Boxers are a nice breed."

The dog was dripping water. And now she shook herself, making a little shower all around her.

"Hey!" said Mr. Allen. "Better put her outside again and let her go home. She's soaking me. And look at the rug."

Sandra took Sally to the door, telling the dog how sorry she was she couldn't stay.

Now she was dogless again. She thought about that problem as she came back into the room. It was odd that neither she nor her two friends, Robby and Ellen, had dogs, while a lot of other people did. When Sandra wanted to play with a dog she had to borrow one.

Sandra looked at her father, her blue eyes wide and questioning. Her dog troubles, of course,

13

were entirely because of him. He was so dear to her and so important—but he was funny about dogs.

He liked only those of established breeds. Knowing all about them was his hobby. He read books about the many kinds, and he went to dog shows. Beagles, boxers, pointers, setters, cocker spaniels—all these he liked. But he didn't have a great deal of money, and he said these dogs were too expensive to buy. And he wouldn't have a mixed dog, not for anything.

Sandra's mother came into the room. She had her new rose-colored suit on and looked nice.

Mr. Allen said to her, "I wish you'd stay home. Your Women's Club committee meeting can't be so important that you have to go out in such a rain."

"Oh, but it *is* important," said Mrs. Allen. "The club's going to try to find a way to make some money so we can have the railroad station painted and fixed up a little. The way it looks now it's a sight."

Sandra and her father agreed with that. The old run-down station did look awful.

14

Mrs. Allen went to the kitchen to get lunch ready. As Sandra heard the light clatter of pans and dishes she began to get hungry.

Her mother called her to set the table, and she was glad to do it. She would be getting that much nearer the good food, and anyway it was her job.

"Mom," said Sandra as she worked, "I really *need* a dog of my own."

"I know," said Mother. "But you know how Daddy is."

Lunch was ready. The family was just sitting down at the table when the telephone rang.

Mr. Allen answered it. And after a moment Sandra heard him say, "Fine. When can I come over?" Again there was a pause while the person at the other end of the line talked. Then they heard Father say, "I'll do that."

He came back to the table, his face bright with a big smile.

Mrs. Allen asked, "What was that call about? You look so happy."

"It's something very, very nice," Mr. Allen said. "You two will like it."

"What, Daddy? What?" Sandra asked excitedly.

Her father said, "It's this. I've always been just about as sorry as you, Sandra, that we didn't have a dog. However, I've been saving up some money. And now I'm going to buy us one—a good one."

Sandra let out a squeal of delight. "Oh, Daddy!" she cried. "We're really going to have our own dog!"

Mrs. Allen was pleased too. "That's great," she said.

16

"I'm getting us a beagle puppy," her father went on, "a very fine beagle."

Mrs. Allen and Sandra both began to ask questions. And Father told them how it had all come about. He said that he had heard from a friend whom he had often met at dog shows that a woman in a nearby town bred especially fine beagles. He had written her to inquire if she had any young ones just now, and it was she who had called up a few minutes ago. She told him that one of her dogs had had five puppies and that he could come anytime he liked and make his choice. Mr. Allen was going to go the first thing next week, so he could get one of the best of the litter. They could not take the puppy home for some weeks though, as it would be too young to leave its mother.

Sandra ran to the telephone and called up Robby, and then Ellen. She told them each the wonderful news about the coming puppy. Her friends were almost as happy as she was, for they knew they would get to play with the new dog too. The three agreed to meet in half an hour if the rain stopped. They would wait for each other under the big maple tree in the next block north

17

of Sandra's house. There they would talk the matter over in detail.

Ellen was much younger than Sandra and the boy, Robby. She was six and a half. But there weren't any other children her age living nearby for her to play with, so Sandra and Robby let her play with them all the time. Anyway Ellen was nice, and she was smart for her age.

When Sandra hung up the receiver, she went to help her father clear the table and put the dishes in the washer.

A car tooted in front of the house. It was Mrs. Mellis, a neighbor, who had come by to take Mrs. Allen to the committee meeting. She was the one who owned the boxer, Sally.

The dishes were soon done, and Sandra again went to the living room to wait for the rain to stop, so she could meet her friends. This time she looked out toward the house next door, where the Olneys lived. They were a young couple who had moved in only a month ago. They both worked and weren't around their place very much in the daytime. They weren't especially friendly either, so Sandra and her parents hardly knew them.

18

The Dog Who Came to Visit

It was quiet over at their house. A lone towel flapped on the clothesline. A bird sat on the fire hydrant beside their sidewalk.

There were flowers growing in Sandra's yard, but there were none in the Olneys'.

Sandra saw a car come along the street. It turned into the neighbors' driveway, and Mr. and Mrs. Olney got out. Mrs. Olney had a brown-and-white spotted dog with her! There had never been a dog at the Olneys' before. He was new.

A dog right next door! Sandra ran excitedly to her father. "I'd like to go over to the neighbors," she said. "They've got a dog, and I want to see him."

"I guess the Olneys won't mind," he said, smiling up at her for a moment. "But how about the rain?"

They went to the window together and saw that the rain had turned into a light drizzle. So that was all right. She put on her raincoat and turned the hood well over her light-brown hair, tucking it in. She hoped she could make the visit to the dog before Robby and Ellen got to the meeting place.

Eagerly, she ran out. She looked toward the left to the big maple. No, Robby and Ellen weren't there yet. She hurried next door, passing under the great old trees that stood along the street, and rang the Olneys' bell.

Plump, young Mrs. Olney answered and asked Sandra into the large, sparsely furnished room.

"I'm Sandra Allen," the girl said. "I live next door. And I saw your new dog, and—" The dog looked at her. His tail began to wave. His eyes looked earnest. Then he ran to her. And as she petted him he turned to pure joy. He waggled all over. His ears flapped. His tail waved wildly.

"Funny, the way he takes to you," said Mrs. Olney. "He usually isn't friendly with people right away."

"He does like me! And I like him," said Sandra. The dog wriggled so that she had to sit down on the floor so he wouldn't bump her over.

He wasn't a purebred dog, but he was very nice-looking. He was medium-sized and lean. His hair was short. His ears were long and floppy, and his eyes were dark and beautiful.

"His name is Chunky," Mrs. Olney said. "He

21

belonged to my great-uncle till now. He called
the dog that for fun because he was always a little
skinny.''

She and Sandra laughed. "That's funny," Sandra said.

Sandra played with the dog a few minutes more.
Then she started to leave, as she didn't want to
outstay her welcome.

22

But Mrs. Olney said to her, "You can take Chunky for a walk, if you like. Put his leash back on. He'll have to get used to the neighborhood before he can run free."

"You sure can walk him all you like," said Mr. Olney, who had been looking on with a rather grumpy face. And to his wife, "You won't get me to do it." He didn't like the dog. Sandra could see that.

Sandra clipped the leash to the dog's collar, and Chunky gave her hand a single quick lick. Sandra thought she had never seen such a lovely dog in all her life.

Proudly and happily she led him outside to the sidewalk. She looked toward the big maple, and saw Robby and Ellen were there now, waiting for her.

"Hi!" she called, running toward them with Chunky. "Look what I've got!"

Robby and Ellen hurried to meet her, talking as they ran. "Where did you get this dog?" Robby asked.

And Ellen said, "I thought you were going to get a beagle puppy."

23

"I am," said Sandra. "But I haven't got him yet. I get him in about six weeks." Then she explained about Chunky, and that she was allowed to walk him awhile.

Robby started to pet the dog, but Chunky drew away and got behind Sandra. From there he looked at the two other children with a questioning look on his gay face, though his tail still wagged a little.

"He doesn't know you yet," Sandra said. "He'll let you pet him when he gets used to you."

Ellen said, "But he's friendly with you, and he only just met you too."

"Some dogs are that way," Robby said thoughtfully. "My father told me about it. They choose a person to like, and they never, in all their lives, like anyone else quite so much. Maybe that's the way it is with Chunky and Sandra."

A glow of happiness filled Sandra. It did look as though it were that way.

Now, the talk again turned to the beagle puppy that Sandra would soon have. It was great that Sandra was really to have a dog of her own at last. The children agreed that Robby and Ellen, as Sandra's friends, would have a share in him, in a way. As they talked, they began to run to give Chunky some exercise.

"This is terrific," said Sandra. "Now I've got this dog to play with while I'm waiting to get my own puppy."

After a while, Sandra took the dog back to the Olneys.

"Come again, Sandra," Mrs. Olney said. "You can play with Chunky anytime I'm here to let you take him. You can sort of help me look after him, if you like. We aren't used to dogs. And we're out so much."

26

2

Chunky Makes Friends

Every evening now, Sandra waited for Mrs. Olney to get home from work. Then she ran over and asked to walk the dog. Mrs. Olney was delighted to hand him over on his leash. And the dog always gave Sandra a quick lick on the nose or hand wherever he could get one in.

And each day, after a run with Chunky, Sandra

brought him into her own house. She wanted her father and mother to get to know him.

Her mother was quite friendly to Chunky, but her father wasn't interested. One day when Sandra brought the dog in, Father paid no attention to him at all. Instead, he began to talk about champion dogs he had seen at dog shows. Then he mentioned the boxer Sally and the wire-haired terrier Friskie, who lived nearby, and asked why she didn't play with them instead of Chunky.

Sandra was disappointed that she could not get him interested in this mixed dog at all. She set out to explain to him how fine—and how unusual—Chunky was.

"Oh, Sandra, honey," her father said, "don't make such a fuss about the Olneys' dog. You'll have your own puppy soon. I've chosen one now, and paid for him. Don't you remember?"

"Of course, I do," said Sandra earnestly. Her heart warmed toward the coming puppy. But then she thought of Chunky again. After all, she had never even seen the puppy yet, and Chunky was here with her almost all the time. She loved him. She said no more, but took him outdoors to play.

Chunky soon began to feel at home in the neighborhood. Then the Olneys let him run free. After that Sandra could play with him any time of day she liked except when she was in school. And much of the time Robby and Ellen were with her and the dog.

Just as Sandra had said he would, Chunky got used to them quickly and was very good friends with them too.

Sandra, Ellen and Robby had been a crowd of three for a long time. Now Chunky became the fourth member of the crowd. Robby and Ellen didn't mind that he still liked Sandra best.

The dog was good at games, and Sandra and her friends had many different ones they played with him. Sometimes they played that Chunky was another child, like themselves. Sometimes they played they all lived on a farm—then he was the horse or mule. Or they were Indians, and Chunky was a buffalo.

The boxer Sally and the terrier Friskie made friends with Chunky too. Often they visited the small crowd. The dogs were always welcome. But now that the children had Chunky they didn't really need to borrow other neighborhood dogs anymore.

Sandra and her mother often fed Chunky a little, because he was so skinny. They thought that the Olneys probably sometimes forgot to give him his dinner. Sandra got an old brush and brushed him almost every day. He liked that, and always stood still.

Mrs. Allen, watching this one afternoon, said, "That dog likes to be neat. And I've been noticing that he's got very good manners in the house. Whoever had him before the Olneys must have been good to him. He's so affectionate and polite."

Sandra was pleased. She brushed Chunky some more.

She was so busy with Chunky and Robby and Ellen these days that she had almost forgotten about the interesting things that had happened at her mother's committee meeting. The day Mother had gone to that meeting, she had come home in the evening and told Sandra and her father the committee had decided to give a play to earn money for the station. They would charge a dollar for adults and fifty cents for children.

Now, over a week later, Sandra was coming home with Chunky one evening. She had been at Ellen's all afternoon, because her mother was at another of her meetings. It was nearly six o'clock when Sandra came to her house. She found her father already there. Her mother came in a moment later, looking happy.

"Guess what?" she said. "We've chosen a play. And they're going to let me be in it! I'm to have a speaking part! Think of it!"

This was truly wonderful. Sandra grew quite excited. She had never seen her mother act, and she could hardly wait till the play would be given.

Meanwhile, Chunky had gone to the refrigerator again and stood before its door, wagging his tail and looking around at Sandra.

Mrs. Allen laughed. "Look at that dog. He's hungry again," she said, and went over and got him some food scraps.

Mr. Allen stood watching. He shook his head. "You're getting him to feel too much at home here. You shouldn't feed him so often," he said.

32

Mother said, "But one can't let him go hungry." She set the dish of leftovers on the floor.

As she leaned over, the dog jumped at her back. "Chunky!" Mrs. Allen cried. She straightened up quickly, and the dog fell to the floor.

He let out a yelp, and Sandra ran and picked him up. She felt him all over to see if he had broken any bones. But he hadn't—he wasn't hurt much at all. Sandra saw that he looked puzzled. That was funny. Why?

Mr. Allen asked angrily, "What on earth's got into Chunky? You, or the Olneys, had better teach him not to do that."

Sandra didn't know what to say, because usually Chunky did have good manners. It truly didn't seem like him to jump on Mom. And he might have hurt her.

Sandra sat on the floor, hugging Chunky, with her cheek against his face.

Her mother said, "You should be scolding him instead of petting him." But then she softened. "I guess he didn't mean any harm."

Sandra now turned Chunky loose, and he went to his bowl and ate.

Sandra and her parents stood watching him for a while. Then her father gave a deep sigh, shook his head and went into the living room.

Sandra waited for the dog to finish, then took him outdoors to play.

Another Saturday morning came—a time to play for long hours. Sandra, Robby and Ellen had planned a fine game with Chunky. But, as it

turned out, they had to give that up because the dog went with his owners for a drive. Sandra had seen him, sitting proud, happy and alert at the window of the Olneys' car.

The children missed him as they sat under the oak tree in Sandra's backyard. They had some boxes with which they often built houses and forts. But they hadn't started playing anything

35

yet. The sunshine was warm. The wind blew gently, and over their heads the green, abundant leaves of the tree rustled.

"Let's play settlers on the prairie," Robby said. "We can do it without Chunky if we have to."

The others agreed. And in a moment, they were making a settler's cabin out of the boxes and looking for unfriendly Indians.

After a while, Robby went to the south side of Sandra's house and pretended that he was plowing with a team of oxen. The girls went close up to the hedge and played picking wild strawberries.

"We settlers just have to get these, or we won't have enough to eat," said Ellen.

Suddenly, Robby hurried over to the girls. "Look," he whispered. "There's a stranger snooping around at the Olneys' house. He looks as though he's spying or something."

Sandra and Ellen peeped through the hedge. They saw a short, rather round, bald-headed man, with his hat in his hand, walking around the house. Now and then he leaned over, shaded his eyes and peered into one of the windows.

36

"Maybe he's a robber," little Ellen whispered.

"Sh—let's stay hidden and watch him," Sandra said.

For a moment the man stood up straight and looked all around him. Then he shrugged his shoulders and went hurriedly to his parked car and drove away.

"He certainly acted strange," Sandra said. "He wasn't *quite* like a robber. . . . But I wonder what he wanted."

Robby said, "I saw him knock on the front door at first. It looked as though he wanted to visit the Olneys. But if he wanted to do that, why did he start peeping in at the windows that secret way? That's what's so strange."

"We'll watch the Olneys' house from now on," Sandra said. "And if that man comes again, we'll have to ask him what he's doing there."

"I'd be afraid to," said Ellen. "He might get angry."

"We'll be careful," said Robby. "Whoever sees him has to call the other two, and then we'll all go together and face him."

38

But days passed, and they did not see him again.

Each day, the friendship between Sandra and Chunky grew. It was amazing how many smart things Chunky did, Sandra thought, and how nice he was.

One of the most important things he did was wait for her in front of her house every afternoon when she came home from school. Then, one day, she found him waiting at a street corner two blocks from the school. And after that he came there to meet her every day. It was wonderful how he always got to that corner at just the right time. It was as though he had a watch.

All the children in the neighborhood knew Chunky by now. And they thought of him as practically Sandra's dog.

"He likes you best, Sandra," said Melissa, a big girl in the fifth grade. "He's practically yours."

"He ought to be hers," said Hal, a tall boy of the same class. "The Olneys don't seem to care about him."

"But Chunky does belong to them," said Robby.

Sandra wished, as she often did, that the dog

really was hers. But then she thought, "He'll always live next door, where I can get him anytime I want. He'll always play with me—all my life."

3

A Terrible Happening

On a warm spring day, Sandra, Robby and a lot of other children were coming home from school. The summer holidays were only about a month away.

"What will you do this vacation, Hal?" Melissa asked.

"I don't know, but I hope Dad will take us on a camping trip," said Hal.

"I'd like to go west," said Robby. "I've never been to the real West."

Sandra said she and her family were going to visit her grandmother when Dad had his vacation.

It was a fine day. Birds were singing more gaily than usual. And all along the street, children were talking, shouting and laughing.

Sandra, Robby, Ellen and the two older children came to the place where Chunky always sat waiting for Sandra. But he wasn't there today. That was strange. The children stopped and waited. They thought Chunky must be late and would come in a minute. But he didn't.

They talked among each other, wondering what could be the matter. And Sandra left the others and began to run, calling him.

Under the trees in front of the Olneys' she stopped and stared in alarm. She could see that there was something wrong with the Olneys' house. There were no shades or curtains at the windows anymore. A newspaper lay scattered on the usually orderly front lawn.

She hurried up the walk and looked into the

house. There was no furniture inside, nor any person. An unused packing box and some scraps of paper lay on the floor of the living room, and there was lots of dust. That was all.

The neighbors had moved out! They were gone. And so was Chunky.

This was terrible. Never in all these weeks had Sandra thought that such a thing would happen.

Robby hurried after her, and she told him. Next, small Ellen came, and then the big children, Hal and Melissa. So Sandra had lost Chunky. It was terrible, they said. After a while, Melissa and Hal walked on toward their own homes, talking about it.

Sandra, Robby and Ellen sat down on the doorstep of the empty house. They were very sad.

Then, away off, they saw a spotted brown-and-white dog, with flop ears. He looked lost and fearful as he trotted along the street. It was Chunky!

"Look!" Sandra cried joyfully, and ran to him. She hugged him and felt him trembling. But he was very, very happy to see her. He wriggled and tried to lick her face. When she let him go he pranced around her and waggled all over. And now and then he stopped and sneezed. Ellen and Robby petted him too.

The Olneys must have left him behind, the three told each other in happy amazement. But how could these people do such a thing?

Robby said, "I guess Chunky *knows* his people deserted him. He's smart. He'd know."

"Of course he does," said Sandra. "Anyway, he must have seen the furniture go off in the moving truck."

"And he saw his people drive off without him," said Ellen.

"Yes. And then he got scared," said Sandra. "But he'll be all right now. He has me and my family to take care of him."

But then, of course, she remembered how her father felt. "But I really know," she added sadly, in a low voice, "that Mom and Daddy don't want a mixed dog like Chunky very much."

Robby and Ellen knew that too.

"We'll hold Chunky while you go and ask your mother if you can keep him," Ellen offered. "Then he won't have to here it if she says no." So they did.

Slowly and doubtfully, Sandra walked to her house. Pushing the front door open, she went in. Her mother heard her and came from another room.

"Oh, Sandra," she cried. "The neighbors moved and left Chunky behind."

"I know. . . ." Sandra started. "Can I—"

"And look," her mother went on, "they stuck this under our front door." She held a note out to Sandra. Then she read it with her:

> Dear Mr. and Mrs. Allen—
> We're moving in a rush. My husband just took a new job in Newark. We can't keep the dog in the apartment we've taken. So we're leaving him to Sandra. He's practically hers already anyway.
>
> The Olneys

"Can I keep him, Mom?" Sandra asked quickly.

"Well," her mother said, looking troubled. "But you know we're getting our puppy. And, anyway, your father—you know how he feels. Let's say Chunky can visit us for a while."

Sandra ran to the screen door, stuck her head out and shouted, "Robby! Ellen! It's all right. Bring Chunky in. He'll stay with me for now."

Robby and Ellen came, with Chunky bounding ahead of them. They were all in the living room in a moment.

Sandra turned to her mother. "Maybe later Daddy will get used to him—and like him—and let me keep him. We could have two dogs— Chunky and the beagle puppy too."

"Sure!" said Robby quickly. "Sure you could, Mrs. Allen."

"Oh no!" said Mrs. Allen. "Two dogs—that's too much! And Sandra, your father's set his heart on a fine dog of an established breed. We have to consider him a little bit too. We'll just take care of Chunky till we find him a home."

Sandra nodded. But she hoped her mother wouldn't be able to find Chunky another home. Then she put the whole miserable thought out of her mind.

She was very excited, because, for a while anyway, Chunky would be hers.

Ellen and Robby stayed a little longer. They followed Sandra and the dog into her room.

"He has to have a place of his own where he can keep his own things," Sandra said.

She gave the dog a corner of her room. Then she put a ball there for him, and an old stuffed bear she hadn't played with for a long time. Robby and Ellen helped Sandra make him a bed with an old blanket.

48

A Terrible Happening

Chunky watched. His pink tongue lolled out on one side. He didn't know what they were doing, but he was happy with them. He was no longer worried and afraid.

That night, when it was bedtime, Sandra's mother wouldn't let the dog lie in his corner of her room. Instead she took Chunky's old blanket and put it in the kitchen for him to sleep on. Chunky lay down on it when Mother told him to. But, happily, Sandra saw in his eyes that he wouldn't stay there.

She went into her room and got into bed. In a minute she heard Chunky's paws on the hard hall floor. He came into her room and lay down beside her bed. Sandra leaned down and patted him.

After a while, she got up and brought his blanket in for him. Sandra felt as though she was wrapped up in a smile as she fell asleep. She was so glad to have Chunky there beside her.

The next morning when she awoke, her father and mother were at her door. And as she looked around, she saw that Chunky had come up on her bed and was lying near her feet. How lovely!

But then Mr. Allen said, "Down, Chunky!"
And Mrs. Allen clapped her hands at him.

Chunky jumped off on the far side of the bed
and tried to hide.

The next night, when they put Chunky in the
kitchen, they closed Sandra's door. They were certainly not getting more friendly toward him. Sandra could see that.

A Terrible Happening

She knew she would have to think of some way
to show them how fine and unusual Chunky was,
if she was to win them over and get them to let
her keep him. She must make a real job of it.

4
Chunky Is Unusual

In the days that followed, Sandra used every opportunity to show Chunky off to her parents. She got him to sleep in the kitchen regularly, as he was told to. He ate neatly, Sandra pointed out to them, and always licked up the few bits he spilled on the floor around his bowl. She got him to jump over a stick when she held it out. That was smart of him.

One day when Sandra was feeding Chunky, her father was standing nearby again. And he smiled a little and said, "Chunky *is* an amusing dog."

At last, Sandra thought, he was softening toward Chunky. She would make the most of this quickly; so she got the dog to shake hands with her.

"See?" she said. "And look, I bet I can make him sit up on his hind legs too." She took the dog's front legs and helped him up. He sat there alone looking pleased with himself. "See?" she said. "Isn't that terrific?"

Her father said, "Honestly, Sandra, that isn't very unusual. I'd like to have a dollar for every dog in the United States who can shake hands and sit up. We'd be rich."

He went off to the living room. Sandra, disappointed, followed. Her mother was sitting there sewing her costume for the play she was going to be in. It was of a silky material that looked golden, and it was going to have a long train, lined with red.

"Have you tried to find someone to take this dog?" Mr. Allen asked her. .

"Yes, but there's not so much of a rush yet, is there?" Mother said.

It sounded good to Sandra that her mother wasn't in a hurry about it.

Now Mother turned the conversation away from the dog. She began to talk about the play and how she and her friends were rehearsing. Then she told about something wonderful that had happened. A man named Mr. Brecker, who had a hall for rent, was going to lend it to her club free for their play. He too was interested in getting the station repaired and painted. And this was how he would help.

It was all very interesting to Sandra. She leaned against her mother's chair and watched her sew. And she began to imagine how fine Mom would look in such a costume. It would surely be a wonderful play. And it would be great to see her mother on the stage like a real actress.

But Chunky's problem didn't leave her thoughts for long.

The next day Sandra and Robby were in front of Robby's house, talking about how to win her father over for Chunky.

Robby thought of a plan to show how smart the dog was. They would go for a long walk with Chunky, he said, and pretend to get lost. Then they would ask Chunky to bring them home. If he did, he would show that he was a lifesaver. And they would have this fine thing to tell Sandra's parents.

Sandra and Robby took some of their money,

all that was left from their allowances, so that if they walked too far they could ride home on a bus. Or so that they could buy some candy if they got hungry. They took Chunky's leash along, to put on him if they came to a place where the traffic was heavy.

Then they set out, with the dog running ahead of them, his ears waving in the wind, his tail high.

They walked a few blocks in one direction, going under the tall trees of their home street, and passing the familiar old-fashioned houses. Then they turned a corner and walked east. They went along this street for a long way and turned another corner. They walked so far they were almost beginning to get tired. Now they came into an area where they had never been before. Here the houses were smaller and new, and much alike. There were many small trees that looked as though they had just recently been planted. It was a new housing development.

They went several blocks into these streets. Then Sandra stopped at a corner.

"This is far enough," she said.

"Come, Chunky," Robby called. "Now let's see if Chunky'll take us back."

But then, looking southward, they saw a big, shiny, new supermarket lying broad and low a few blocks farther on.

Their eyes lighted. They smiled. They jingled the coins in their pockets. And they told each other they would go there and take a look at this place and buy some candy. At the thought of that they both grew desperately hungry. They called Chunky, who had gone to sniff a tree trunk, and hurriedly walked on with him.

When they got to the doors of the supermarket, they put Chunky's leash on, and joining several grown people who were just entering, they went in too.

The place was not crowded, and they walked

up one aisle and down another with Chunky close beside them. And they looked at everything. There were canned goods, ice cream, soaps and wash powders, loaves of bread and cookies.

They were looking for the candy section. And after a while, they saw candy right next to the shelves where the paper napkins and towels were. There was a tall stack of napkin boxes on the floor. It was about five feet high. They were hurrying past this and toward the candy section when a man in a white jacket, who worked there, came up to them.

"No dogs allowed," he said firmly. "Take him out." And he grabbed at the leash as though to put Chunky out himself.

Chunky was afraid of the stranger. He jumped away, and bumped into the tall stack of packages. They tumbled down over him and all around him and a little on Sandra and Robby too.

The dog yelped. And Sandra squealed.

The man was angry. "Now look what he's done!" he shouted at them.

Robby said quickly, "We'll stack them all up again."

But the man said, "No, just get out with your dog, and stay out!"

Sandra pulled Chunky by the collar, and Robby pulled on the leash and they got him out the nearest door.

"Oh, Robby," said Sandra when they were safely out in the street. "That was awful. We did something terrible, knocking down those packages."

"But we didn't break anything," said Robby.

Neither of them blamed Chunky for bumping into the stack. It was their fault for bringing him into the supermarket, and the man's fault for scaring him.

They walked a few steps away. But now they remembered about the candy. They wished they had been able to buy some before they got out, but they didn't dare go back.

Sandra looked around her. Then, she cried out, "Oh, Robby, we came out a different way from the way we went in. And now I'm all turned around. I think we're really lost."

Robby looked north, south, east, west. To his surprise, he too was confused.

"What will we do?" Sandra was a little frightened. "We'll have to ask someone how to get back to our street. And maybe we'll have to take a bus home then," she said.

But Robby was against that. He said, "Let's not do that. Let's do what we planned. We'll see if Chunky can lead us home."

"Okay," Sandra said. She knelt down before the dog and told him, "We're lost, Chunky. Take us home."

The dog didn't know what she meant. He just cocked his head and looked at her questioningly.

"We're lost," Robby repeated. "Chunky, you have to save us."

But still Chunky didn't do anything. He just stood waiting and wagging his tail.

Finally Sandra had an idea. "Let's go home and eat, Chunky," she said. "Eat!"

Chunky understood that. He began to bark happily. He ran around them trying to make Sandra start walking home. When she didn't, he trotted off a little way and stopped and waited for her and Robby to follow. Then he ran on.

Sandra and Robby smiled at each other. "It's going to work!" said Robby triumphantly.

They ran and skipped after him. They followed him for quite a distance, and he brought them back to the familiar houses of their own neighborhood. Finally, they were back at Sandra's house.

Here, the dog barked again and hurried to the front door.

Robby and Sandra rushed indoors with him, and stood before Sandra's parents in the living room.

"You know what Chunky did?" Sandra asked jubilantly, proudly. And she and Robby told the whole story of that afternoon, even about the packages that were knocked over in the supermarket. But, of course, mainly they told about how much smarter Chunky was than they were. He knew the way home when both of them didn't.

Mother shook her head. "That is not unusual for a dog," she said gently. "Most of them have a good sense of direction, although some do get lost once in a while, of course."

"That's how it is," said Father. Then he opened his newspaper and began to read.

Sandra and Robby went outdoors together. "We're stupid," Robby said. "We should think of something better to show Chunky off."

"We'll have to," said Sandra. "Pretty soon I'll get the beagle puppy, and then Mom and Dad will make me give up Chunky for sure—unless we can show them he's very unusual. We've just got to do something, and fast."

Robby looked sad. "But what if he isn't really very unusual? What if he's just average smart, and nice?"

5
Fine Days and Bad Days

As the night when the play would be given drew near, many people of the town were very busy. The women and the husbands who had acting parts rehearsed more and more often. Others sold tickets from door to door or took orders for them over the telephone.

Some of the husbands and sons made scenery. They also made a big curtain that could be drawn up and down in front of the little stage. Sandra's father helped with these things too, and he was very good at it.

Mrs. Allen had to rehearse more often in the afternoon now. Sandra kept on going to Robby's or Ellen's house then.

Once, however, she stayed home, and a sixteen-year-old girl came to stay with her for a few hours. She sat in the living room and played the radio and did her homework. And she kicked off her shoes and kept pushing her hair out of her face.

Sandra watched her for a while and then went out in front of her house. Robby, who was riding his bicycle up and down the sidewalk, put it down on the grass of her lawn and pulled out a comic book from under his belt. They read it together. Then Ellen came over. She brought her doll carriage with a worn-out doll in it. And she carried a rather big roly-poly clown under one arm.

Robby said, "We don't want to play with those things, Ellen." He thought, as he often did, that Ellen was really too young for him and Sandra. Still, he did like her.

66

Sandra thought Ellen's things were fun. She put the big, round clown into the doll carriage and laughed at the way he stuck out on all sides.

If this was the way the girls were going to play, Robby wanted none of it. He went away.

Ellen rolled the carriage down the walk. Chunky, who had been off sniffing a telephone pole, came racing back, his face eager and gleeful. Reaching Ellen, he got up on his hind legs and bumped the handle of the carriage with his front paws.

"Chunky!" Ellen cried, "stop that!"

Sandra drew the dog away.

"He was going to upset my carriage," Ellen said indignantly.

But Sandra said, "He didn't mean to. He was just playing." She turned the dog loose, and right away he bumped at the carriage again.

Ellen grew angry. "He's doing it on purpose," she said. "He's bad today."

"He's not bad," said Sandra, angry too.

She and Ellen began to quarrel over it. And Ellen took her things and went home.

Sandra held Chunky affectionately. "You shouldn't have done that," she told him softly.

That evening, she told her parents about it. "Ellen gets mad too easy," she said, "but I don't know why Chunky did that to her carriage."

"That's playing rather rough. It's odd for such a polite dog as Chunky," her father said.

Sandra was pleased at the gentleness of her father's tone. She would make the best of this mood of his. Quickly, she put Chunky through his routine of shaking hands and sitting up, to show once more how well behaved he was. Afterward, she rolled on the floor playing with him. The dog and girl were very happy.

But then Sandra's father gave a little cough and said to her mother, "We simply must get someone to take this dog off our hands. Sandra's getting much too fond of him. And the longer we wait the harder it will be for the two to make a break with each other."

"I've been asking around," Mother said, in a troubled voice. "But I haven't found anyone yet who'll take him. And we can't just throw Chunky out or send him to the public dog shelter."

"No, of course not," Father agreed. "But do try harder to get him placed."

Sandra didn't say anything. She was just grateful her mother hadn't found anyone who wanted Chunky.

After supper, Mrs. Allen brought out her sewing box and started to work on her costume again. And she talked about the rehearsals and the play. She didn't think any one of the crowd was a very good actor or actress. "Of course, I'm as bad as any of them," she added.

"You'll be all right, after you get a little more practice," Mr. Allen said.

"I don't know," said Mrs. Allen. "Still, it's fun putting on a play."

Sandra wasn't worried about the play at all. She knew it would be just great. She went to the window that overlooked the house where the Olneys used to live. And then she gave a little gasp at what she saw. "Oh!"

The round man was there again! In the evening light, she saw him walk up the front path and ring the doorbell. Then, he saw that the house was empty. At that, he threw up his hands. And he made a face that showed both surprise and shock.

Sandra ran to the phone and called Robby and then Ellen and told them the round man was here.

They said they would come immediately, so that they could question the mysterious man.

Then, she dashed outdoors to meet her friends. But in a moment she saw that they were already too late. The man was gone. He had gotten into his car while she was phoning, and now he was driving away again.

"Oh, goodness," she said to Robby, who got to

her first. "Now maybe we'll never know what he wants or who he is."

"It's too bad," said Robby.

"I bet he's a robber," said Ellen.

Saturday night—the night of the play—came at last. Many of the neighbors had bought tickets. They did it because they liked the women of the club and because the show was for a good cause. They also did it, as Sandra's father pointed out, because the tickets didn't cost very much—not half as much as some other benefit performances.

Sandra was very excited. And so, in a quieter way, were her parents.

Mother's gorgeous costume was laid out on her bed. Sandra went into the bedroom several times to look at it. There were red slippers with gold trimming to wear with it. Lovely! And in only two hours her mother would be wearing this costume out on the stage in front of all the people!

Just before supper, Mr. Allen sat down to read his newspaper, as he always did. Sandra got out her crayons and started to draw a picture of Chunky. She would hang it over her father's desk, so he would get more and more used to the dog.

The telephone rang, and Mrs. Allen went to answer it. She talked on the phone for quite a while.

When she hung up, she looked upset. "Well, I have news," she said to her husband and Sandra. "I phoned this woman earlier today. And she just called me back to say she has decided."

"Decided what?" Mr. Allen asked. "You're not making yourself clear."

"Yes, I know," Mother said. "That's because I know Sandra won't like the news. And, honestly, I don't like it much either."

Sandra looked up questioningly.

"It's about Chunky," Mother went on. "I've found someone—this woman on the other side of town—who will take him off our hands."

Sandra made a grab for Chunky. "No!" she cried.

"This lady is quite old. And she doesn't want another dog much," Mother went on, "but she

73

said if we just couldn't find anyone else to take him, she'd make a good home for Chunky. She's very fond of dogs—all kinds of dogs."

Sandra said miserably, "We're not really going to give Chunky away? We couldn't. He's our friend, and he's so used to us. And if that lady lives at the other end of town, I'd never even see Chunky anymore! Please Mom! Daddy! Please don't. . . ."

"Daddy, could we let her keep him?" Mother asked.

But her father turned to Sandra and said, "Don't make it so hard for us. We don't want two dogs—we told you that all along. And we've already bought the beagle puppy. We'll pick him up tomorrow. And now that your mother's found a good home for Chunky, we'll go through with it. Okay?"

Sandra picked up the wriggling dog and hurried off to her room with him. His lanky legs dangled as she ran. Tears trickled down her face.

Just before she shut her door, she heard her mother say, "Oh, John, it's really pretty cruel to take Chunky away from Sandra. They love each

other. They're absolutely attached to each other. It surely doesn't matter that much about the breed."

Her father was talking in a low voice, and Sandra could not understand him. She glanced back and saw that he looked upset. She shut her door quickly. She knew there was no hope there.

Sandra's attempts to show her parents how smart and valuable Chunky was had been too small. She had failed. To them Chunky seemed to be just an ordinary dog, like any other of the mixed breeds.

Miserably, she petted Chunky. He sensed her unhappiness and didn't know what to make of it. So he gave a little whimpering sound and licked her hand. Then he pranced around her, as though to cheer her up.

Sandra didn't say anything when her mother called her to come to supper. She wiped her tears and ate silently. But food didn't taste very good tonight. Her mother and father talked a lot, mostly about the play. They kept off the subject of the dog entirely.

Sandra did not want to go to the play now. But

76

she had looked forward to it for a long time. Besides, she knew that her mother would be terribly disappointed if she did not go. And this thing about Chunky wasn't really Mother's fault. Again, tears came for Chunky.

Mother said that they must get ready to leave for Brecker's Hall. Then she put an arm around Sandra's shoulders and asked her to hurry.

Sandra went off and washed, combed, and put on the dress her mother had laid out for her. Her mother came and helped her button up. And she suggested that Sandra leave Chunky outdoors tonight while the family was away. That way he could run around and amuse himself, she said, and would not get lonely.

Sandra said she would do that. She knew Chunky would not run away. He liked her too much.

Then Mother took the car, put her costume in the back seat and drove to the hall alone. She had to get there early to dress and put makeup on before the audience arrived.

Sandra and Chunky stayed in her room awhile. And she thought about Robby and Ellen. They

would be horrified at her losing Chunky. But tomorrow she would have to tell them.

Sandra's father called her. "Let's go on over now and see Mom's show," he said.

So they set out. They would walk, for it wasn't far to the hall. When they left the house, Chunky of course thought he was coming too. But Sandra told him to stay home, and he trotted back, sat down in the middle of the front walk and looked after them.

Sandra started to point out to her father that Chunky was very well behaved. But she stopped and said nothing. A few tears trickled down her face again.

It was rather dark under the trees, and the street lamps made big pools of light. Here and there, a few people came out of their houses. Some of them walked in the same direction as they.

Father and daughter went along silently. All the while, Sandra still tried to think of something she could do to make him let her keep Chunky. But no idea came to her at all.

6
A Good Show

As Sandra and her father came near Brecker's Hall, they saw the strings of lights hung out in front. These made a big patch of brightness on the lawn and sidewalk.

More and more people were coming toward the hall. A little crowd stood before the building, and some people were already inside.

Sandra's father gave the lady at the door their tickets, and they went in and found seats near the front. They sat on folding chairs brought in for the occasion. At first, Sandra was too sad to pay much attention to the people around her.

Mr. and Mrs. Danfred and Mr. and Mrs. Costa, people from the Allens' own street, were sitting next to them. They said good evening and talked to Mr. Allen.

Sandra began to look around and saw some of the kids she knew in the audience. There were Hal and Melissa and some of the younger kids from her school, with their parents. And then Robby and Ellen arrived with their families. Soon, practically everyone Sandra knew was here.

She thought about Chunky and slid deep into her chair, her mouth curved downward.

Now the lights in the hall were lowered, the curtain went up and the play began. It was about an ancient European court in the days of kings, queens and knights. All the actors were dressed in colorful velvets and silks. Sandra didn't understand quite everything that was said, but she thought the play was wonderful. Her mother didn't appear. She would come on in the second act.

When the curtain went down, everyone clapped politely. Then a murmur of talk went up.

"They're pretty good for amateurs," said one woman nearby.

"Acting takes talent as well as a lot of real professional training," said a man.

Sandra could tell he didn't think the play was very good. She was sorry, because her mother and her friends had put so much hard work into it. She herself still thought it was fine. And, loyally, she was a little angry at the man.

She asked her father what he thought. And he was loyal and enthusiastic too. "It's great. Very good," he said. And Sandra felt a little better. She looked at her friends in the audience. They were all enjoying the play.

As the second act began, everyone watched with expectation to see what would happen next. Sandra's mother came on stage now. She looked lovely in her costume with the long train. She

stood still and spoke her lines. She did it well, and seemed only a little nervous.

Sandra glanced away from the stage for a moment. She was proud of her mother, and she looked toward Robby and Ellen again to see how they liked the play now.

Just then, a gasp and a murmur went up from the audience; Sandra quickly turned around again —and she saw something awful. Chunky had got in somehow and was on the stage! He must have come in from the back door.

Now, as Mother swept across the platform in her fine costume, he saw her, and he did a strange thing. He went to her and sat on the train and rode along with her as she crossed the stage. The audience broke into hearty laughter and clapped.

Sandra was horrified. Chunky was ruining the show—and especially her mother's part. It was awful. And the actors, and especially her parents, would be furious at Chunky. She must rescue him. Quickly, she ran backstage.

From the wings, she saw Chunky take the center front of the stage for himself. He stood up on his hind legs, and it looked just as though he were

85

bowing to the audience. Everyone clapped and cheered louder.

"Chunky!" Sandra called from the wings. "Chunky! Come here!" And the dog left the stage and ran to her, waggling all over.

She grabbed him and scolded him, but he did not seem to understand that he had done anything wrong. He actually seemed pleased with himself.

Sandra was very sorry about what had happened, but she had to protect Chunky from the actors. They would be very angry at him for spoiling their play.

She picked him up and took him back to her seat with her. There she held him tightly in her lap. She dared not look at her father.

"That dog," Mr. Allen said, thoroughly annoyed.

The show had stopped. The actors were waiting for things to quiet down. But the excited laughter and chatter in the hall continued.

A man from one of the back seats got up and came hurrying down to the row of chairs where Sandra and her father sat. It was the mysterious round man the children had seen at the Olney house!

86

"Excuse me. I'll be just a moment," he said, looking up at the actors on the stage. Then to Mr. Allen and Sandra, "This is the dog I've been trying to find. I'm a sort of guardian to him. I have the right to see he's well taken care of. And I have the right to say who can have him."

Chunky recognized him and began to wriggle happily, trying to get to the man.

But Sandra was holding him more tightly than before. She thought, "So the round man is Chunky's guardian. He isn't a robber or anything like that." The mystery of what he had been doing around the Olneys' house was solved. He had been looking for Chunky. But what would happen now?

The round man was saying to Sandra and Mr. Allen, "May I speak to you after the curtain goes down?"

"Certainly," said Mr. Allen.

"And by the way," the man went on. He turned to the rest of the audience, "This is a partly-trained stunt dog. Very smart. Getting on the lady's train that way—that was a funny bit he was taught to do in an act he had. If you'd like it, he

87

and I will put on a little show for you after the play is over tonight. Shall we?"

"Yes!" and "Sure!" and "That would be fine!" people from the audience answered.

Robby called out, "Sandra, Ellen and I always knew Chunky was smart!"

"You bet he is," the man said. And then to the audience, "I'll do it. I'll give you a show with the dog."

He went off, saying he had to collect a few things for Chunky's act. Then he went out of the hall.

The actors got into the right places on the stage again, and the show went on. Now they were playing to a cheerful audience. Everything went even better than before. When the curtain went down for the last time, the people clapped very heartily.

The round man came in with several objects under a cloth and went backstage. A murmur of voices arose in the hall. People were full of curiosity about the man and the smart dog. Some stood up and craned their necks to get a better look at Chunky. Sandra's father looked at him with interest and amazement.

Chunky sat upright and alert on Sandra's lap, an eager look on his face. And Sandra, stroking him, didn't know what to think or how to feel. She thought the man might take the dog away from her. He might take him himself instead of letting the elderly lady from across town have him. Then she thought, what was the difference, if she couldn't keep him?

Now the round man came out of the wings at the side of the stage, carrying a hoop.

He said, "Okay. We're ready." And to Sandra, "Turn the dog loose, little girl."

Sandra did. The man whistled just once, and Chunky, wagging his tail mightily, ran to the stage and quickly jumped up on it.

The man roughed him up affectionately. Then he said, "Ready?"

He touched Chunky on the head, and the dog stood on his hind legs. The man then introduced himself as Mr. Mullins and gave Chunky's name for those who did not know him. Then the show began.

Mr. Mullins swung the hoop and threw it into the air. Chunky watched, and when it was just low enough, he jumped through it without knocking it down.

Everyone clapped and exclaimed. So they did the act three more times.

Next, Mr. Mullins put Chunky on a round wooden stool and asked him to sing. Chunky sat up on his hind legs and made as good a song as he knew how.

The people laughed happily.

The man put Chunky on the floor and, standing a little distance in front of him, leaned over. Chunky immediately jumped lightly to his back and licked the man's ear.

"Hey, Sandra!" said Mr. Allen, laughing. "Chunky was probably trying to do that stunt with Mother the time he jumped on her when she was going to feed him."

"Sure," said Sandra. "Of course he was."

The round Mr. Mullins now brought out a doll carriage from the wings. "Here," he said to the dog. "Take the doll for a ride."

Chunky got up on his hind legs, and with his forepaws pushed the carriage around the stage.

The audience clapped again. Above the sound,

Sandra could hear Ellen yelling, "That's what Chunky was trying to do with my doll carriage the other day! And I didn't understand."

Sandra's heart glowed with pride in Chunky. The show was over. Chunky and the man took a bow again. Then Chunky, through with his job, raced off the stage and back to Sandra.

91

Both Mr. Allen and Sandra petted and praised him.

"A fine dog," said Mr. Allen. "And I never knew it."

The round man smiled, and called out to them, "Looks like you've been good to him," and he looked at Sandra.

The people of the audience began to leave. Mrs. Allen went away to take off her costume and put on regular clothes. Mr. Allen and Sandra waited for Mr. Mullins in the aisle.

Mr. Mullins came to them in a moment, and Mr. Allen told him his and Sandra's names. Then the man told them his whole story. A good many other people, including Robby and Ellen, Melissa and Hal, and their families, crowded around and listened too.

It seemed that Mr. Mullins had been the closest friend of Joe Harker, a professional animal trainer, who was eighty-seven years old this spring. He had been training Chunky for TV and the stage but had not gotten very far with it when he died, a few weeks ago.

Before that, Mr. Harker had called Mr. Mullins

in one day and had asked him if he would act as a sort of guardian to the dog when he, the old man, passed on. He wanted him to make sure Chunky would be well cared for and loved. Though the dog wasn't fully trained for the stage yet, he would make a fine, smart pet.

After the funeral, Mrs. Olney, a niece of Joe Harker's, had asked to take the dog. And Mr. Mullins had consented, thinking that as a relative she had a right to him. He himself couldn't take Chunky, as he already had four dogs of his own.

But he had never felt quite right about giving the dog to the Olneys. So he had gone to their house twice to take them by surprise and see if they were treating Chunky right. The first time, the Olneys weren't home and the dog was nowhere in sight. He peered into the windows to see if Chunky was inside, but he wasn't. So he left. The second time, he saw that the Olneys had moved, and he assumed, of course, that they had taken the dog with them. So he left again. But he was still worried about Chunky.

Mr. Allen then told him that he and his family lived next door to the Olneys, and that they had

seen that the Olneys were not much interested in Chunky. He told how attached to Sandra the dog had become. And he explained about the way the Olneys had left the dog to them with a note when they moved, without first asking if they wanted him.

"Do you want him now?" Mr. Mullins asked, looking at Sandra.

"Yes!" said Sandra. "Oh yes, I want him."

And her father said yes too. "We'd like him very much," he said. "He's really quite a dog. I'm afraid I didn't let myself appreciate him before, because I had my mind fixed on a beagle puppy we had bought that we're getting tomorrow. But we'll just have two dogs now. That's all."

Mrs. Allen had finished dressing and had come up behind Sandra. She had listened too. "I'm glad we're going to have Chunky," she said softly. "And the lady across town doesn't really want him anyway."

Chunky was standing close to Sandra, wagging his tail and lolling his tongue out at one side.

Mrs. Allen patted him and said, "You helped us give the audience their money's worth in entertainment tonight, Chunky." Then she said to the others, "Come on, let's go home now. It's getting late." To Mr. Mullins she said, "Do come over and visit us and Chunky whenever you like. You'll want to know how he's getting along."

"Thank you, I will," said Mr. Mullins. "I'd like to."

Sandra had been thinking only of Chunky all this time. Now she remembered about the beagle puppy who was coming tomorrow. She thought, "Chunky and I will like him. And maybe Chunky will teach the puppy some of his terrific stunts."